This igloo book belongs to:

Emilie

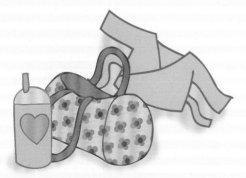

iglOObooks

Published in 2019
by Igloo Books Ltd
Cottage Farm
Sywell
NN6 0BJ
www.igloobooks.com

GUA006 1218
2 4 6 8 10 9 7 5 3
ISBN 978-1-78670-675-1

Written by Sienna Williams
Illustrated by Cathy Hughes

Designed by Kerri-Ann Hulme
Edited by Stephanie Moss

Printed and manufactured in China

The Princess Ballet

igloobooks

Once there were three best friends
who all loved to practise ballet.
After **spinning**, **twirling** and **jumping**,
they made a wish one day.

"How we long for our dream of performing to really come true, and dance in front of princesses in a **magical** land, too."

PING! Suddenly, the friends got a **wonderful** surprise, as a princess ballet school appeared before their eyes.

"Join us!" said the teachers.
"Point your toes, **twirl** and **sway**.

There's a show for two princesses, and you'll **dance** in it today."

At the royal palace, the princesses prepared for the show.
Sophie strung up **twinkly** lights that set the ballroom aglow.

Charlotte baked some cupcakes that were **tasty** and **sweet.**
"Yum," said Cook, "those treats look good enough to eat!"

Suddenly, the excited pets
chased around the room.
SMASH went the decorations as
they whooshed by. ZOOM!

"Naughty pets!" cried Charlotte. "We can't have the show now."
"Oh yes we can," said Sophie. "Let me show you how."

Sophie watered all the flowers,
then turned to Charlotte and cried...

... "Look, the gardens are so pretty.
We can have the ballet show outside!"

Charlotte was so excited. The pets jumped up and down.

They all knew this was sure to
be the **best** performance in town.

Meanwhile, the dancers **tapped** their
feet and **swayed** from side to side.
They all tried hard to balance and
held their arms out wide.

But they still felt worried about
dancing in front of a princess.
The teachers told them not to worry,
as their moves were sure to impress.

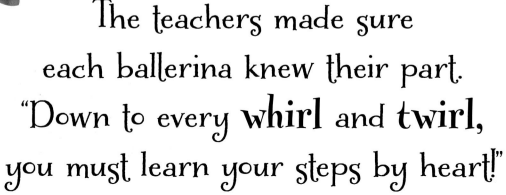

The teachers made sure
each ballerina knew their part.
"Down to every **whirl** and **twirl**,
you must learn your steps by heart!"

They **leaped** and they **jumped**.
They **whirled** and **twirled** some more!
When it was show time,
they couldn't wait to hit the floor.

Soon, the palace gardens were ready.
When all the work was done,
the princesses couldn't wait to
have some ballerina fun!

Charlotte admired her new cake,
as a carriage **swept** down the drive.
"Look, Sophie!" she cried. "The ballerinas
are starting to arrive!"

The guests **twirled** round and round,
and shiny stars **twinkled** in the sky.

They were so excited as
the ballerinas **waltzed** by.

"This way, everybody," said Sophie, with a grin.
"Please take your places. The show is about to begin!"

The princesses cheered as the ballerinas **leaped** and **twirled**.
They moved across the stage, as their sparkly tutus **swirled**.

The friends had so much fun. It was the **best** show ever.
The greatest thing of all was that they'd done it together.